The Adventures of

Rodger Dodger Dog

Jan Britland

Illustrated by Mike Swaim

ISBN-13: 978-1463715595

ISBN-10: 1463715595

I dedicate this book to my youngest grandchildren, Rory, Aidan, Dalton, Duncan and Kaci. And to my older grandchildren who can now read it to their children.

Also to my daughter Kelly for pushing me to follow through and bring Rodger Dodger Dog to life!

My husband Bill for "getting it" and last but not least to Mother who totally thinks it's a great idea!

Talented Dog

Rodger Dodger is a dog,
a handsome dog is he.
Rodger has a talent for
he can climb a tree.

Rodger climbed
the tree one day
and much to his
surprise...

5

He came up eye-to-eyeball
with someone else his size!

Soon the fur began to fly and
a lot of noise was made.

After the war
was over
dear old Rodger
he was dazed.

**For Rodger had never fought before
and he never will again.
Now that the war is over he and
Mack the cat are friends!**

Clever Dog

Rodger Dodger is a dog,
a clever dog is he.
He knew he was a clever dog
the day he went to the sea.

Rodger went to the sea one day
and while walking on the sand,
a fish jumped up so high
he bounced onto the land.

11

The fish flipped and rolled around
while gasping out for air.
Rodger rushed to his side and
looked on with despair.
He asked the gasping fish,
"Why don't you walk back to the sea?"

The fish gasped and said to him,
"Do you see feet on me?
I have fins and I can swim,
but walk I cannot do!
And if I dry, I will die,
so now it's up to you!"

Rodger thought and he came up
with a truly clever plan.
To help the fish get to the sea
and off the dry sand.

He told the fish, "Bite on my tail and
I'll tow you back to the sea."
"Great!" said the fish.
"This will be fun for you and fun for me!"

15

So off they go the fish in tow,
down to the water's edge.
And when they went in up to his fin,
the fish, he did begin to swim.

The fish then said,
"Thank you my friend
for getting me back to here.
I think the world should crown you...

The Strongest Dog

Rodger Dodger is a dog, the strongest dog is he. Rodger was the strongest dog until he met...

...the flea!

Rodger met the flea one day
while digging in the park.
When the flea first bit him
poor old Rodger he did bark!

The flea ran up and down his back
and bit him with such force,
when the day was over
dear old Rodger he was...

...Hoarse!

**Finally the flea did sleep
as for Rodger not a peep!
When the dawn started breaking
dear old Rodger started shaking.**

**Rodger bit and scratched and rolled
but nothing seemed to help,
when the flea bit him on the neck,
dear old Rodger he did yelp!**

25

Rodger rubbed against a tree
and dashed across the street.
The only part that didn't itch
were the soles of Rodger's feet!

Rodger jumped and rolled and
dove into his neighbor's pool.
But the flea he did hang on
he was really cool!

Rodger ran to the porch and
rubbed flat against the mat,
when he was through he glanced up
that's when he saw Mack the cat.

Rodger knew what he must do
to rid himself of the flea,
so he got up and dashed down
to sit beneath his tree.

Mack, now curious,
came over to see Rodger,
who was an awful mess,
something he couldn't avoid
while under so much stress!

The flea was really
quite upset by
Rodger's new condition.
The only place fit to ride
was sitting up between
his eyes!

So when Mack, a fluffy cat,
came strolling into view,
the flea was thrilled to see
someone neat and clean and new!

So the flea he did leap, as fleas can do, several feet... he landed down on Mack.

Rodger ran and left the scene before he could jump back!

For Rodger knew Mack,
that fluffy cat was truly
fully equipped with a collar
and some powder to get
rid of the flea real quick!

FLEA·NO·MOR.
X-TRA STRENGTH FLEA COLLAR

**Rodger Dodger is a dog,
the strongest dog was he.
Now he is the smartest dog
because he beat the flea!**

The End!

Look for Rodger's Other Adventures!

A Christmas Story. Come along with Rodger and his pals as they pick out their first Christmas tree. After decorating it with handmade ornaments and opening presents Christmas morning they realize that of all the gifts you can get Friends and Family are the best! It is sure to become a Christmas favorite!

Rodger Saves Bunny. When Rodger comes across Bunny passed out in the woods he decides to take Bunny home to nurse him back to health. When Bunny wakes up Rodger finds out Bunny is terrified of him. What Rodger learns is a shock to him. Find out what Rodger learns and how he fixes his friendship with the terrified Bunny!! Your children will delight in their new found friendship.

Rodger Meets Dr. Glee. Rodger wakes up one day not feeling well at all. His tongue feels very large, his head feels very small. His tummy does a flip flop, his brain it feels fuzzy, he knows he needs help when his hearing goes all buzzy. Find out what is wrong with Rodger and how his friends get him to the zoo to see Dr. Glee. It is sure to delight your child!

You can play the "Help Rodger Find His Friends Game,"
or contact Jan Britland at: www.rodgerdodgerdog.com

Made in the USA
San Bernardino, CA
13 May 2014